For all the children who come to Nethercott, Treginnis and to Wick
M. M.

For Norman and Jen
S. U.

FARMS FOR CITY CHILDREN
Nethercott is one of three farms run by the educational charity Farms for
City Children. Every year three thousand children come with their teachers to spend
a week living and working on the farms. They come in all seasons, in all weathers.
Now more than ever it matters that children can experience life in the countryside.
Calves are born, sheep are shorn and chicks and ducklings hatch. And this is
not something the children just watch. They feed the hens, hiss at the geese and
hear owls hoot in the night. They are the farmers.
Michael Morpurgo

First published in hardback in Great Britain by HarperCollins*Publishers* Ltd in 1996
Published in this edition in Great Britain by HarperCollins *Children's Books* in 2021

HarperCollins *Children's Books* is a division of HarperCollins*Publishers* Ltd.

1 3 5 7 9 10 8 6 4 2

ISBN: 978-0-00-833508-3

Text copyright © Michael Morpurgo, 1996
Illustrations copyright © Sam Usher, 2021

Visit our website at: www.harpercollins.co.uk

Printed in Italy

The BIRTHDAY DUCK

Written by
michael morpurgo

Illustrated by
Sam Usher

HarperCollins *Children's Books*

Sam didn't want to go to the farm.

"You'll like it when you get there," said Sam's grandad.

"I won't," said Sam. But he knew he had to go. **Everyone** in Mrs Southerden's class was going. Besides, Grandad said it would be **good** for him.

"**City boy** like you can get a lot from being on the farm. Fresh air, fresh eggs. I wish I could go myself. You'll be back on Friday for my birthday. We'll have a party."

Grandad waved **goodbye**.

Sam watched from the back of the coach till he couldn't see him any more. It was a whole **week** before he would be home again. Sam did his best not to cry.

It was a **long**
way to Devon.

Motorways turned to roads,

roads turned to **lanes,**

narrow lanes with **grass**

growing down

the middle.

Suddenly ahead of them was a **huge** house, like a palace, with green fields and trees all around.

"That's Nethercott," said Mrs Southerden from the front of the bus.

"We're here. And what are you now?"

"Farmers!"
they chorused.

And so they were. Up with the dawn
and out to **work**.

Milking **cows**,
       feeding **horses**
             and **pigs** and **calves**.

And the **sheep** had to be fed too.

All before breakfast.

Breakfast was **steaming porridge,**

scrambled **eggs**

and all the **toast**
you wanted.

Then there were
sheds to **muck out**,

hens and ducks and
geese to **let out**,

eggs to **collect**.

There was even a **bull**,
but you weren't allowed in
his field, just in case.

Sam didn't have **time**
to miss Grandad.

They worked **all** afternoon too and even then it wasn't
finished. In the evening the cows had to be milked again –
and do cows make a mess!

The **lambing sheep** were

brought into the barns for the night,

the pigs **fed,**

the horses **groomed**

and the hens and ducks and geese
shut up in case the **fox** came
skulking up the lane.

Sam worked like a Trojan,
ate like a **king** and slept like a **log**.

The farmers were **kind** and smiling, especially
the old gardener who brought the vegetables to the
kitchen. He had silver hair like Sam's grandad.

Sam **loved** every minute of it.

Even when they had to muck out stinky sheds
or clear a field of **stones** so the corn could grow
through in the spring.

But best of all was when a lamb was born,
warm and wet and steaming in the frosty air.
He watched her breathe her first breath,
walk her first step,
drink her first milk.

He had so much to tell Grandad.
Only Lisa didn't enjoy it.
"My feet hurt, miss. My back aches, miss.
It's cold, miss."
All week she never stopped moaning.

Tuesday was market day.

It was the first thing Sam **hadn't** liked. In the auction there was a red-faced man who twisted the calves' tails to make them move. He even kicked them, and all the time he laughed like a drain.

Sam couldn't bear to watch him.

He went outside and looked at the ducks and chickens instead. They huddled together in the backs of their cages. But one of them, a lovely snowy **white duck,** stood by the wire and quacked at him. Sam touched his soft feathers with his finger.

"Out of my way!" It was the red-faced man. "That's my supper you're looking at." And he grabbed the duck by the feet.

"You're not going to **eat him!**" cried Sam.

"You can't!"

"You got a better idea?" laughed the red-faced man. Sam didn't have to think about it. "I'll buy him off you," he said, and he took out all his money. "I've got five pounds."

"It's a deal," said the red-faced man.
He took the money and Sam was left
cradling the duck in his arms.

What was he going to do with him?

What would Mrs Southerden say?

Quickly, he slipped the duck into his sports bag.

"No quacking," he whispered.

"Please!"

All the way home to Nethercott he wondered **what** to do.
He walked at the back well away from the others, just in case.

There was only **one** place he could think of to hide him: in
the shed in the vegetable garden. No one would know, if he
was **careful,** if he was lucky.

The duck stood in his shed and looked about him.
He seemed to like it. "You'll need some straw for a bed,"
Sam told him. "And some food."

"And water," came a voice from behind him. It was the
old gardener. "Duck's got to have water," he said. "Where
d'you get him?"

"Market," said Sam. "This man, he was going to kill him."

"Was he now? Well, we can't have that, can we? I've got
some sandwiches in my shed, and milk. Will that do?"

So they fed him together.

"It's a drake," said the gardener.
"We'll call him Francis, shall we –
you know, like the famous sailor –
Francis Drake?"

"No one knows I've got
him," said Sam.

"I won't say a word," said the
old gardener, tapping his nose.

For the rest of the week the children worked hard on the farm and nobody guessed that Sam had **a secret**.

On the last night there was a crackling bonfire and everyone sang songs and ate too many sausages.

Sam went off to be with Francis, and the old gardener was there already.

"What you going to do with him?" he asked Sam.

Sam had worked it all out. "Birthday present for my grandad. He'll be seventy tomorrow."

"Same age as me," said the gardener. "He's a **lucky** man – to have a grandson like you."

Next morning the old gardener was waiting for him in the shed.

Together they settled Francis deep down in his sports bag.

"Good luck," said the old gardener.

Sam ran for the coach. He wanted the back seat, in the corner. That was the safest place. If Francis **quacked** just once, that would be it. He waved goodbye to the gardener until he couldn't see him any more.

They only stopped once.

"Lunch," said Mrs Southerden. **"Everyone out."**

Sam didn't want to leave his bag behind, but Mrs Southerden said he had to. When he'd finished his picnic he ran all the way back to the coach.

Someone was there before him. Lisa was bending over the back seat.

"It quacked," she said. "You've got **a duck.** I'll tell."

Then Lisa was running up to the front of the bus.

"Miss, miss, Sam's got **a duck** in his bag."

Quickly, Sam took Francis out of his bag and hid him under his coat.

"Don't be silly, Lisa," said Mrs Southerden. "All week you've been nothing but a nuisance. And now you're telling silly tales. Come and sit at the front with the sickies, come on."

"But, **miss**," Lisa cried. "It's true. He's got a duck, **honest**."

Everyone looked at Sam.
He shrugged his shoulders,
sighed and held his bag
up, upside down.

Lisa's mouth opened
and shut, just like a
goldfish.

Sam just smiled sweetly.
But it was a **very** long
journey home.

Sam couldn't **wait** to see Grandad. He ran up the steps to the flat.

"I'm back, Grandad," he cried.

He made Grandad sit down
with his eyes **closed**,

while he ran a **bath** for
Francis to paddle in.

Then he called Grandad in.

"For you, Grandad," he said.

"Happy birthday."

And he told Grandad all about Francis and the red-faced man
in the market and the old gardener down at Nethercott.

"That's a lovely, lovely duck," said Grandad, shaking his head.

"But, Sam, we can't keep him up here in the flat.

Wouldn't be right."

"Why not?"

"Listen, Sam," Grandad said. "A duck needs a pond.
He needs friends too, like you, like me. And he needs
his **freedom.**"

All evening Sam tried to persuade Grandad to keep
Francis. But it didn't do any good.

"We'll talk about it in the morning," said Grandad.
"Get some **sleep** now."

Grandad got him up early
the next morning.

"What's up?" Sam asked.

"**You'll see,**" said
Grandad.

They set off with Francis in Sam's sports bag, his head peeking out. There was no one else about.

"Where are we going?' Sam asked.

"You'll see," said Grandad, a twinkle in his eye.

They were walking through the park in the early morning mist, when Francis quacked.

Suddenly there were other ducks quacking, and ahead of him Sam could see a great dark lake and ducks swimming towards them. There were geese too, and moorhens and swans.

They crouched down by the lake and let Francis go.
He waddled into the water, settled himself, flapped his
wings, shook his head and cruised out to join his friends.

"Well," said Grandad,

"what do you think?"

"I suppose we can always come and feed him," said Sam.
"**Every day** if you like," said Grandad. "Look at him,
Sam. That's a very happy duck and I'm a very happy man.
You know, I said you'd get a lot from being on the farm,
but I didn't think you'd get **a duck.**"

Sam laughed.

"You enjoyed it, though? The farm?" said Grandad.

"It was the **best** week of my life," said Sam.

"But it's quite nice to be back with **you**."